Aria

André W. Renna
7/19/21

ducky

To Aria, my very special grand daughter, who has been my inspiration.
Her imagination, smile, and laughter brings joy and happiness to all.

To my children, Chris , Christine and Jamie and ,my sister Veronica,
your insights and support have been invaluable. To my grandson Aiden,
I look forward to your stories.

And to my wife Pat, who encouraged me to pursue my dream.
Thank you for being by my side the entire journey. —AR

Always for my girls. —DL

Published by Papa Publishing
2129 Quail Drive
Lancaster, Pa 17601
www.papapublishing.com

ISBN 978-0-578-90395-8

Printed in the United States of America
First Edition, 2021

Visit Aria and Ducky at: AriaandDucky.com

The Adventures of Aria & Ducky

the Surprise Birthday Party

Aria and Ducky met one afternoon when Aria was one year old.
Aria won Ducky at a boardwalk game during a family vacation at the beach.
They have been "best friends" ever since and enjoy many adventures together.
Adults see Ducky as a stuffed toy...
but Aria knows he is special and comes to life when adventure calls!

Aria and Ducky have been best friends for as long as Aria could remember.
They had grown up together having many great adventures.

But today was a very special day: it was Ducky's birthday.
Aria was planning a big surprise party to celebrate.

Everyone would be at the party: Penguin, Turtle, Unicorn, Flamingo, Snakey and T-Rex. It would be a party that Ducky would remember forever.

Aria asked her mommy if she would help to get all the decorations and food. The house would be decorated with balloons, streamers and a big "HAPPY BIRTHDAY DUCKY!" sign.

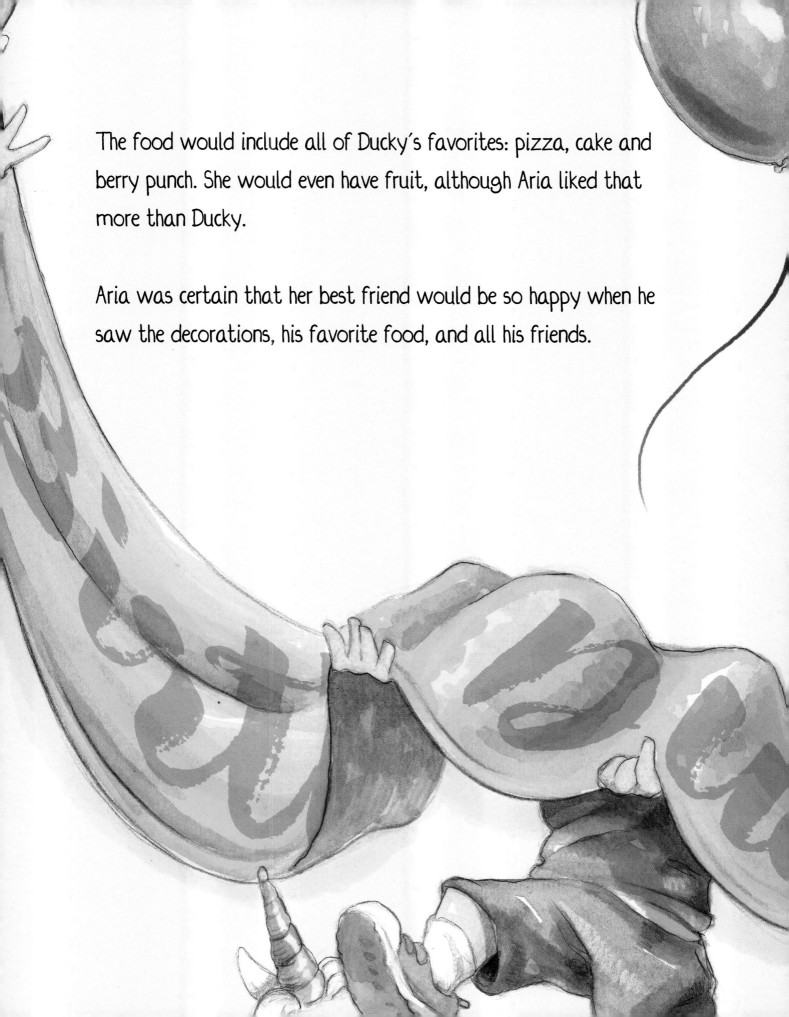

The food would include all of Ducky's favorites: pizza, cake and berry punch. She would even have fruit, although Aria liked that more than Ducky.

Aria was certain that her best friend would be so happy when he saw the decorations, his favorite food, and all his friends.

Everything was planned. Now she had to make sure Ducky was not at the house until the big surprise. Aria and daddy would take Ducky to their favorite place to play.

Aria asked Ducky if he would like to go to the playground
with her and her daddy.

Ducky smiled from ear to ear, jumped up, and said,
"Sure, that would be great." So, they walked to the
playground together.

Aria and Ducky went on the slides, seesaw, merry-go-round, swings and all the other play areas at the playground. Daddy watched as the two friends had so much fun.

As they played, Aria was careful
not to mention Ducky's birthday.
She wanted to really surprise him,
so she acted like she did not remember.

Aria noticed that Ducky seemed quieter, and not as cheerful as usual. She asked him if he was feeling ok. Ducky did not want Aria to know that he was disappointed that his best friend had not remembered his birthday, so he just said, "I'm fine, let's keep playing."

Ducky thought his best friend had forgotten his special day.

Back at Aria's house, mommy and the friends decorated
and set the table. The food was due to arrive soon.

When the preparations were finished, the friends left the house.
They planned to be back in one hour so they could jump up and
yell "surprise" when Aria and daddy brought Ducky to the party.

At the playground, daddy told Aria that it was time to go. He gave her a wink and she winked back. She knew that soon her best friend would be so surprised. They started the walk back to Aria's house.

Meanwhile, the guests returned to Aria's house.
When they opened the door,
they could not believe their eyes!
And Unicorn shouted...

The decorations were torn down, the table setting scattered everywhere, and the cake had been eaten.

Then Penguin noticed Jasmine, the cat, sitting under the table licking frosting off her paws.

"Oh no!" yelled T-Rex, "Jasmine has ruined the party!"

They knew that Ducky would arrive any minute. There was no time to fix the mess and make another cake. The friends were certain he would be disappointed.

Just then, the door opened and Aria and Ducky walked
into the house. Aria yelled, "Surprise, Ducky! Happy Birthday!"
But no one else shouted. They were still just staring
at the mess made by Jasmine.

Ducky looked at Aria with a very puzzled look.
He said, "What's going on?"

Aria replied, with a sad look on her face, "This was supposed to be a special birthday party for you, but someone ruined everything. I'm sorry Ducky."

Ducky looked at the torn decorations, the food mess, and all his friends. He then turned to Aria with the biggest smile and said," Don't be sad, Aria, this is the best birthday ever!"

"I thought everyone, even my best friend, had forgotten my birthday. But you didn't. You planned a special day for me. I don't need decorations, cake or even presents. I am here with all of my friends and especially you, Aria, my best friend ever!"

Aria smiled, gave Ducky a big hug, and said,
"You are my best friend always and forever, Ducky,
HAPPY BIRTHDAY!"